P9-DTU-043

topps® LEAGUE Story

JINXED!

· BOOK ONE ·

By **Kurtis Scaletta**

Illustrated by **Eric Wight**

SCHOLASTIC INC.

ISBN 978-0-545-55089-5

Copyright © 2012 by The Topps Company, Inc.
All rights reserved. Published by Scholastic Inc., 557 Broadway, New York, NY 10012, by arrangement with Amulet Books, an imprint of Harry N. Abrams, Inc.
Topps and Topps League are trademarks of The Topps Company, Inc. Amulet Books and Amulet Paperbacks are registered trademarks of Harry N. Abrams, Inc.
SCHOLASTIC and associated logos are trademarks and/or registered trademarks of Scholastic Inc.

12 11 10 9 8 7 6 5 4 3 2 1   13 14 15 16 17 18/0

Printed in the U.S.A.   40

First Scholastic printing, January 2013

Book design by Chad W. Beckerman

For Byron, who proves I'm lucky.

Special thanks to Sean, T.J., and
Dylan of the Saint Paul Saints.
—K.S.

To Ethan & Abbie.
—E.W.

1

I was just a kid, but I already had my dream job. I was the batboy for the Pine City Porcupines. The Pines were the baseball team in my hometown. They played in the Prairie League.

I wrote them a letter in the off-season, asking if I could be a batboy. I told them that I would love to do it, that I knew a lot about baseball, and that I would work really, really hard.

Dad said I should also send them a résumé.

"What's a rez-u-may?" I asked him. That's how he said it: "rez-u-may."

"It's a list of all your past jobs and your accomplishments," he said.

"I've never had a job."

"Good point," my dad said. "But you do have a lot of accomplishments."

So I got on the computer and typed up my accomplishments. It took me all day.

CHAD SNYDER

EDUCATION
- I am a student at Pine City Elementary School.

JOBS
- If you hire me, this will be my first job.

ACCOMPLISHMENTS
- I have more than 5,000 baseball cards.
- I have kept score at every baseball game I've attended since Uncle Rick showed me how.
- I learned every Porcupine player's name last year.
- I walk and feed the dog without being reminded (except by the dog).
- I won the coach's award in Little League.
- I collected cans to raise money for the Pine City Animal Shelter.
- I have my own résumé.

"I've never seen 'I have my own résumé' on a person's résumé before," Dad said when I was done.

"But I worked really hard on it."

"Good point. It looks great. Let's mail it tomorrow."

• • •

I waited two weeks, but nobody called.

"It can take a long time," said Dad. "Be patient."

I waited two more weeks, and still nobody called. I was beginning to give up hope.

"The season hasn't even started yet," said Dad. He was right.

Then I got the call! The Porcupines wanted me to come in for a job interview.

I put on my best pants, my good shoes, a shirt with a collar, and a snap-on tie.

"You look great," said Dad. "Remember to speak clearly and make good eye contact."

"OK."

"Do you want a ride?"

"No. I'll feel more grown-up if I ride my bike." We lived really close to the ballpark.

• • •

I talked to the clubhouse manager, whose name was Wally. He had a big white droopy mustache that covered his mouth. At least I could make good eye contact.

"You have an impressive résumé," Manager Wally said.

"Thanks. I wrote it all by myself."

"Why do you want to be a batboy?" he asked.

"I love baseball," I told him. "You should see my room. I have posters and pennants on all the walls. I also have over five thousand baseball cards in binders. They fill a whole shelf."

"I love bacon, but I don't want to work on a pig farm," replied Wally.

"Yeah, but being a batboy is fun," I said.

"Sometimes it is, sometimes it isn't," said Wally. "It's always hard work. Have you ever done hard work?"

I thought about the hardest work I'd done. I'd pulled weeds in the garden. I always did my homework on time. I walked our spaniel mix, Penny, and cleaned up after her.

"All the time," I said.

"Final question," said Wally. "Explain the infield fly rule."

I knew all about the infield fly rule. My uncle Rick told me about it. Uncle Rick has told me almost everything I know about baseball. I explained to Wally that the infield fly rule kept the infielder from cheating and turning an easy out into two easy outs.

"I've always wanted somebody to explain that to me so I could understand it," he said. "When can you start?"

"When school gets out," I told him. Dad had been very clear about that.

"Great," said Wally. "But no more ties. Don't you know that there are no ties in baseball?"

"No ties," I repeated. I could totally keep that promise.

2

"Why don't we talk about our plans for the summer?" said our teacher, Ms. Singer, on the last day of school.

Here was my chance to tell everyone about my job. I hadn't told anyone yet. I was scared the Porcupines would change their mind. I thought Wally might call and say, "Sorry, kid, we couldn't wait for school to get out. We're bringing in a kid who's dropped out."

But now I knew my batboy job was for real. I would be starting the next day. There was no game, but Wally said I should show up and help unload the team bus.

I decided to wait until everyone else had talked before I told the class my news. You should always save the best for last.

"Who wants to be first?"

"Me! Me!" cried Abby.

"Yes, Abby?"

"I have an acting role," Abby said. "It's going to keep me superbusy, but it's an awesome opportunity."

"That's great," Ms. Singer said. "Can you tell us more about it?"

"Sorry," said Abby. "I can't."

"Are you in a play here in Pine City?" asked Emily. "Can we come see you?"

"I can't tell," said Abby.

"Give us a hint," said Ivan.

"Well, it's a very challenging role," said

Abby. "It involves both improvisation and pantomime."

"Huh?"

"Those are acting terms," Abby explained.

I didn't know what her acting role was, but my news was probably better.

One by one, the other kids in the class talked about their summer plans. Oscar's family was going to South Dakota to see Mount Rushmore. Michelle was taking ballet lessons. Scott was rereading his favorite fantasy series. Crystal was playing softball in the park league. (That was cool, because softball was practically the same thing as baseball.) Maria was going camping. Rachel was expecting a baby brother. (OK, that was hard to top. But I still thought I had the coolest plans.) Jayden didn't have any plans except bike riding and swimming.

"There's nothing wrong with that," said

Ms. Singer. "It's better than watching TV and playing video games."

"That's what I'm doing!" said Ivan. The whole class laughed.

The other kids took their turns until Dylan and I were the only two left.

I didn't know Dylan that well. He sat with other kids at lunch. He didn't raise his hand a lot, but when the teacher called on him, he usually knew the answer. He was good in gym class but not a show-off.

He didn't raise his hand now. Maybe he had some awesome news he was saving for last, too. Whatever it was, it wasn't as awesome as my news.

Ms. Singer looked back and forth at him and me, waiting for one of us to talk.

I really wanted to go last. I crossed my arms and looked at Dylan. "Your turn," I mouthed.

He gave in.

"I'm going to be a batboy for the Pine City Porcupines," he said. "I start tomorrow night."

Every kid's mouth dropped open, but nobody's mouth dropped more open than mine.

Everyone started asking a million questions.

"Are you going to hang out with the players?" asked Oscar.

Dylan was cool about the whole thing. "Of course."

"Will you go on road trips?" asked Crystal.

"Nah. I just work the home games."

"What will you do?" asked Ivan.

"All kinds of stuff," said Dylan.

"What's the big surprise?" Jayden asked.

"Huh?"

"I heard about it in a radio commercial. Saturday's game . . ."

". . . is Kids Get In Free Day!" Ivan blurted out.

"Yeah," said Jayden. "And the radio said to come for the big surprise."

"I don't know about any surprise," said Dylan.

"Do you get to wear a uniform?" Oscar asked.

"Yep."

"Wow," said Oscar.

"Do you get paid?" Maria asked.

"Of course."

"How much?"

"N.O.Y.B.," said Dylan.

"I'm a batboy too!" I shouted.

Everybody looked at me.

"Well, I am," I said. "For the Porcupines."

"Sure you are," said Oscar.

"Everybody's a batboy!" said Ivan.

"I am, and I can prove it!" I said. "Just come to Kids Get In Free Day. You'll see."

"I was already going," said Ivan.

"Me too," said Crystal.

"Everybody's going," said Oscar. "Are you going?"

"I'm a batboy! I have to be there!"

"Chad, don't raise your voice," said Ms. Singer.

"Sorry."

The bell rang, and school was over. Not just for the day but for the whole year.

3

ylan and I showed up at Pine City Park the next evening to unload the bus, just like Wally asked. It was beginning to get dark. The bus wasn't there yet, so we waited. Dylan was quiet.

"This'll be a fun summer, huh?" I asked.

"Sure," Dylan answered—but not like he meant it.

"The Pines lost three games in Centralville and two out of three in Farmington," I said. "They're in last place by nine games."

"Oh, well." Dylan shrugged.

"I wonder what the surprise is on Saturday?" I said.

"Something to do with baseball, I bet," Dylan said.

"Hey, do you collect baseball cards?" I asked.

"Nope."

I wanted to tell Dylan about my collection, but decided not to. I stopped trying to talk to him. He didn't want to talk to me anyway.

The bus finally rolled in. There was so much mud spattered on it that you could barely see the porcupine logo on the side.

The first player off the bus had a mustache like an old-timey movie star. He was new to the team, but I recognized him. It was the Pines' new pitcher, Lance Pantaño.

"Good evening, gentlemen," he said, with a little bow. Then he leaned over and whispered, "Be careful. There's a giant rat on the bus."

"A *rat*?" I took a step back.

"Just be careful," Pantaño said. With that, he turned and walked across the parking lot toward the players' entrance.

I looked back at the bus and saw Sammy Solaris coming down the steps. Sammy was usually the designated hitter. He could really smack the ball, but he was too slow to play in the field.

"Have you seen the rat?" he asked in a low voice.

"No," said Dylan.

"Keep your eyes open," said Sammy. He poked his thumb at the bus. "Huge . . . rat . . . in there . . ."

"Really?" said Dylan.

"Hey, Sammy! Chad the batboy," I jumped in. "I'm a big fan."

"You're a big fan, and he's a big player. All

those corn dogs, eh, Sammy?" said the next guy off the bus. It was Wayne Zane, the catcher. Zane's face was as wrinkled as an old mitt. He had been with the Porcupines for as long as I could remember.

"*You're* the corny one," said Sammy. It was true. Wayne Zane was always joking around.

"I'm just sayin'," said Wayne. "But seriously, kids—watch out for that rat."

Both players set off for the locker room.

Wally came out to the parking lot. He opened the side door of the bus and pulled out a cart.

"You kids haul in the equipment," he said. "No dillydallying."

Dylan pulled out a canvas bag of bats, set it on the cart, and reached in for another.

"What's dillydallying?" I asked Dylan.

"I think it's like lollygagging," he replied.

"Oh."

Dillydallying? Lollygagging? Must mean talking instead of working. I knew baseball had a lot of funny words. I wondered if these were two of them.

I started pulling out equipment, but I kept my eyes on the bus door.

One by one, the rest of the team hopped off and headed for the locker room. There was Ryan Kimball, the tall, tattooed closer.

"Have you seen the rat?" he asked us.

"No," said Dylan.

"Keep your eyes open," Kimball said. "And watch your toes."

"EEEK, EEEK, EEEK!"

"EEK! EEK!"

Outfielders Danny O'Brien and Brian Daniels scurried past us making rat sounds. They looked so much alike, you never knew who was playing right field and who was playing left.

"*Pssst.*" George "President" Lincoln, the really serious-looking second baseman, tipped his head back toward the bus and tapped his nose once. He gave us a solemn look as he walked past.

"I'm not scared of rats," said Dylan.

"Me, neither," I agreed.

"I've seen them at the pet store," he said. "They're cute."

"Yeah."

Of course, a wild rat would be scarier than a pet-store rat. I wasn't about to run off, though. There was one player I was still watching for: a big blond guy with a smile like you'd see in a toothpaste commercial. I wanted to meet him.

Another guy came off the bus. Here was a Pine I didn't know. He yawned, blinked, then looked at us.

His nose was all black.

There were whiskers on his face.

His baseball cap had big round ears attached to it. They looked like they'd been cut out of a brown paper bag and stuck on with duct tape.

"Hi, there. I'm Tommy Harris." He offered his hand. "I just got called up from rookie league."

I stared at him.

Dylan blinked.

"What's wrong?" asked Harris.

"Um . . ." said Dylan.

"You've got rat stuff on your face," I told him.

"And ears," Dylan added.

Harris turned around and looked at himself in the bus's side mirror. "Oh, man. That's what I get for falling asleep on the bus." He found a handkerchief in his pocket and wiped at the eye black on his nose and face. "It's tough being the new guy."

"I guess that's the rat," said Dylan. "The ones at the pet store are cuter."

"Is there anybody else on the bus?" I asked Tommy.

"I don't think so," he answered. "Why?"

"I want to meet Mike Stammer. I have his baseball card, and I want to ask him to sign it."

"You must've missed him," said Tommy.

"He'll be in the locker room, though." He headed that way, still rubbing at the whiskers.

"Minor leaguers have baseball cards?" asked Dylan.

"Most don't," I said as I struggled with the last overstuffed bag and put it on the pile. Dylan started pushing the cart. The load wobbled, and I put a hand on it to steady it. "Mike Stammer was in the big leagues for a while."

• • •

We rolled the cart into the equipment room and started to unload it. Dylan worked twice as fast as me. I hoped he didn't think I was dillydallying. I was just slow.

"That's everything," I said.

"Yep," said Dylan. He waved and left. I was sure he was still mad at me.

I popped into the locker room one more time.

"Is Mike Stammer around?" I asked Wayne Zane.

"He dropped off his stuff and went for a walk," said Wayne. "He said he wanted to be alone."

That was too bad, I thought. But Mike would be here tomorrow. I hoped so, anyway. In minor league baseball, a player can get called up at any time. He can also get cut at any time.

"If you stick around, he'll probably be back," said Wayne.

I looked at the clock. Mom and Dad had told me to get home as soon as I could.

"I'd better not," I said. I thought of something I'd meant to ask earlier. "Hey, do you know what the surprise is at Saturday's game?"

"Nah, nobody tells us anything." Wayne

swung his locker door closed. "I just hope it's not a surprise retirement party for me."

"No way," I told him.

"Just sayin'," Wayne said.

I got my bike and started for home. I had not gone far when I slammed on the brakes. Something was pawing at the ground in the shadows by the right field wall. What was *that*? My heart raced. I turned my handlebars so my bike light pointed that way. I hoped it was only a big dog and not a coyote or bear or something.

The shadow stopped and turned toward me.

It looked up at me in surprise.

I looked back in just as much surprise.

Huh?

ike Stammer jumped up and brushed the dirt off his knees. His big toothpaste-ad smile gleamed in the lamplight.

"Hey, there," he said.

What was he up to? Looking for worms? Maybe he was going fishing the next morning. Or maybe he was in the middle of some weird exercise routine. In any case, at least Mike wasn't a coyote!

"Uh, hey, there. I was just looking for you, and, uh . . . will you please sign a baseball

card?" I said quickly as I got off my bike. I pulled the card out of one pocket and a pen out of the other.

Mike took the card, held it flat in his left palm and scribbled on it. "You probably wonder what I'm doing crawling around out here, huh?"

"Nope," I lied. "It's none of my business."

"Good kid. Hey, what's your name? I'll get you tickets to tomorrow's game."

"My name is Chad, but I don't need tickets. I'm a batboy!"

"Great. Glad we finally got one for the summer." Mike gave me back the card. "So you won't tell anybody about this?"

"No way."

"Thanks."

I got back on my bike and pedaled off. I glanced in the mirror and saw Mike crawling around in the grass again. I hoped he didn't scare anybody else, because he cast one big shadow!

• • •

"How did it go?" Dad asked as soon as I got home. He looked up from his book, which was about Madagascar. Dad was interested in everything. The last book he read was about eggplant farming, and the one before that was about the Franco-Prussian War.

"It was fun," I said. "Wayne Zane is funny. At least, he *tries* to be funny. And there's a new guy named Tommy Harris who's really friendly. He fell asleep on the bus and they put a rat face and ears on him. Mike Stammer is nice but kind of weird. And Sammy Solaris is even bigger up close."

"Did you work hard?" Dad asked.

"Of course." I thought about how Dylan

was way faster than me, but maybe he was just superfast.

"Saturday is Kids Get In Free Day," Dad told me. "I heard an ad on the radio about it."

"I know, but I don't have to worry about getting into the game free. I get *paid* to be there."

"The ad said there was going to be a big surprise," said Dad. "Do you know what it is?"

"No. Everybody's talking about it, though."

"Maybe the surprise is that you're the new batboy," said Dad.

• • •

As soon as I got to my room, I took a binder off my shelf and slipped Mike Stammer's card back into the plastic sleeve. The binder was just for players who'd played for the Porcupines. I had over forty of them.

I have other binders, and even more baseball cards in boxes. I have cards going all the way back to the 1950s, when my grandpa started collecting them. He gave his baseball cards to Uncle Rick, and Uncle Rick gave his—and Grandpa's—cards to me. Some of them were tattered at the corners and had worn spots on the face. Others were still perfect, even though they were twenty or thirty years old. A few were worth a lot of money, and a lot of them weren't. I didn't care. I loved them all, whether it was a Hall of Famer or a guy who was only in the majors for one season, like Mike Stammer.

I flipped the sheet over to see the back of Mike Stammer's card. The stats don't lie. Mike was a good hitter and runner. He wasn't enough of a slugger to DH, but he got on base a lot. If only he played shortstop as well as he hit, he'd be back in the big leagues. He just made too many errors.

I didn't need the card to tell me that. I'd seen Mike on *Baseball Bloopers* plenty of times. I'd seen him run at a ball and accidentally kick it like a football. I'd seen him throw the baseball right over the first baseman's head.

That's why Mike was back at Single-A. He had to work on his game. I hope he did get better . . . but not right away.

The Porcupines played the Heron Lake Humdingers on Friday night. They also played them on Saturday and Sunday afternoons. Wally told Dylan and me to show up two hours before each game started. I wanted to get there even earlier.

On Friday, I biked to the ballpark and saw the patch of grass where Mike Stammer had been crawling around.

Suddenly, I realized what he had been looking for.

I jumped off my bike to find it.

When I walked into the locker room, it was exactly four o'clock.

"You're late," said Wally.

"I'm right on time!" I pointed at the clock. The minute hand was right on the twelve.

"If you're not five minutes early, you're late," said Wally. He went off to the equipment room.

"If he wanted us here at five to, why didn't he say so?" I asked Dylan.

"I don't get it, either," he replied.

He was wearing a Porcupines uniform with *BB* on the back. Our uniforms were here!

I found my own uniform on the bench and changed into it. The pants were tight around the waist and so long in the legs that I had to roll up the cuffs, but I swelled with pride. I was one of the team!

"I was hoping for the porcupine logo," said

Dylan. One of the Pines' logos was a fierce porcupine. Our caps had the other team logo, an interlocking *P* and *C* for *Pine City*.

"I like the porcupine one better too," I told him.

The uniform was pretty cool.

"Yech!" someone shouted from the other side of the locker room.

Tommy Harris pulled a glue trap out of his locker. "Very funny, guys!" he said.

"We heard there was a rat on the loose," said Wayne Zane.

Mike Stammer was getting dressed too. He started to put his socks on.

"Those are the smelliest socks I've ever smelled," said Wayne Zane.

"I haven't washed them in eighteen days," said Mike. "I'm trying to break the jinx."

"Maybe you can break the jinx by *washing*

those socks. In extremely hot water. With bleach."

"But the last time I had a jinx, I broke it by *not* washing my socks," said Mike. "I just can't remember how many days it took."

"Don't wash them, then," said Wayne Zane. "But don't wear them, either. Bury them . . . deep . . . *very* deep!"

"Here's a clean pair," said Sammy. He tossed two socks over to Mike. "Try these—do us all a favor."

"Ah, it's probably not the kind of jinx that socks can fix, anyway," Mike said. He put on the clean pair.

That reminded me. "Hey, Mike, I have something for you." I dug through my street clothes and found the four-leaf clover in my shirt pocket. It had taken me half an hour to find it. I handed it to Mike. "I figured that's what you were looking for last night."

"Yeah, it was," he admitted. "I've had so much bad luck lately, I'm willing to try anything. But I couldn't find one." He tucked the clover into his pants pocket. "Thanks, uh . . . Chad, right?"

"Yep."

"I hope this works!"

"Me too." I didn't really believe in four-leaf clovers, but it didn't hurt to try. "You want me to, uh . . . get those?" I pointed at the unwashed socks.

"Don't touch 'em, kid!" said Wayne Zane. "Not without a hazmat suit."

It was time for batting practice, which everybody called "BP." The batters took turns, swinging at easy pitches. Dylan and I ran around in the outfield to gather up the balls.

They call that "shagging," but I don't know why. Just another one of those weird baseball words. I just know it's fun.

The Porcupines' mascot walked by, waving at the fans who were there early. "Hey, Pokey!" I shouted. The giant porcupine saw me and waved. His back quivered. The quills looked sharp, but I knew they weren't.

"Yours," said Dylan. I turned just in time to see a ball bouncing straight at me. I fielded it and threw it back toward the pitcher's mound. Last year I'd seen the batboys and thought those kids were really cool. Now some kid was looking at me and thinking the same thing.

Wally walked into the dugout when BP was over.

"I need one of you to help out the visiting team," he said.

"What?" I dropped the last ball back into

the canvas bag. "You want us to help the other guys?"

"That's why we have two batboys," Wally said. "One for here, and one for over there. The other teams do the same for us when we go to their ballparks."

"Oh," I said. That made sense, but I still didn't like it much.

"So who wants to volunteer?" Wally asked.

I traded looks with Dylan. He was a better batboy, but I really wanted to hang out with the Porcupines.

"Well?" said Wally.

"I'll do it," said Dylan. He didn't look very happy about it.

"Great. Thanks for being a good sport," said Wally.

"Thanks," I said as Dylan headed off to the visiting team's dugout. He didn't even look at me. Now he probably thought I was a dillydallier *and* a bad sport. Maybe I should have volunteered to help the Humdingers.

"You know how to set up a bat rack?" Wally asked.

"Sure." I didn't, but I could figure it out.

"Here's the lineup card. Go do it, and hustle."

I did figure it out, and I hustled.

Tommy Harris led off the bottom of the first inning for the Porcupines. He paused just before he got into the batter's box, checked his shoelaces and batting gloves, pulled up his socks, and straightened his jersey. He rubbed the tip of his bat and nodded to it like they had a secret agreement. Finally, he got into his batting stance.

Tommy drew a walk. The next two batters struck out, but Tommy stole second base. The pitcher was so surprised, he didn't make the throw and Tommy slid in safely.

The Humdingers' pitcher chewed his lower lip. Beads of sweat rolled down his neck. He threw a couple of balls and then a curveball that didn't curve. Sammy Solaris knocked it out of the park. The Porcupines were up by two runs! I got to trade high fives with Tommy and Sammy when they came back into the dugout. It was awesome.

Being up close, I knew something that the fans didn't: Tommy was partly to thank for that home run. He stole second base right under the pitcher's nose, and that shook up the pitcher. I never would have seen how nervous the pitcher was if I was sitting in the stands.

I loved my new job!

• • •

That was the only scoring for either team until the seventh inning, when the Humdingers had runners on second and third. There were two outs. The batter swung and grounded a ball right at Mike Stammer, who was playing shortstop. It should have been an easy out. Mike got the ball and wheeled to make the throw to first base, but his feet got tangled up. He fell down, and the ball rolled into the outfield. Both runners scored—and just like that, it was a tie game.

"Early season jitters," Wayne Zane told Mike during the seventh inning stretch. Wayne took off his mask and shin guards and chest guard, and put them on the bench. It was his turn to bat.

"I've had the early season jitters for eight weeks," Mike said.

"Hmm. That *is* a long time," Wayne admitted. "Maybe you've really got the June swoon."

"I've had it since last July," said Mike.

"Well, then. It must be a two-summer slump."

Mike glared at him.

"Just sayin'." Wayne headed to the on-deck circle for his practice swings. I stayed on the bench. I saw Mike getting a cup of water.

"I could have gotten that for you," I said.

"Afraid I'll drop it?" Mike joked. He swigged the water and refilled the cup.

"I'm supposed to help out," I said with a shrug.

"Sorry your clover didn't work," said Mike. "It'll take a seven-leaf clover to break this jinx."

"Have you tried a rabbit's foot?" I asked. I'd seen one in the junk drawer at home.

"Nah, that grosses me out," he said.

"Me too," I admitted.

"You just gave me an idea, though," said Mike.

• • •

The Humdingers scored three more runs and won the game. The Pines' fans were slow and quiet as they trickled out of the ballpark.

"Come back tomorrow afternoon for Kids Get In Free Day," the announcer, Victor Snapp, said over the PA system. "Be sure to get here early and secure your seat for the second game against the Humdingers, and see the big surprise that the Porcupines have in store for you." I wondered if Victor knew what it was. I wished I could run up to the booth and ask him, but I was still helping the team.

I put the bats away while Grumps, the Porcupines' manager, told off the team. His real name was Harry Humboldt, but everybody called him Grumps. Lots of guys in baseball have nicknames. The funny thing about Grumps was that when he was a player, his nickname was Happy Harry. I even had his major league card from the 1980s. He had a big grin. Managing must have made him grumpy.

"I've seen better fielding from six-year-olds!"

Grumps shouted. He didn't name names, but he looked at Mike Stammer. "You can't give a team extra outs, especially when you're not scoring that many runs. That's why we're in last place by nine games."

"Ten games," said Wayne Zane. "I saw on the scoreboard that the Rosedale Rogues won again."

"Nine games, ten games, it's still early in the season," Grumps replied. "Just don't get into a hole you can't dig yourselves out of."

"And the first rule of holes is, when you're in one, stop digging," said Wayne Zane.

"That's right," said Grumps. "So stop digging!" He marched out of the locker room.

Everyone was quiet for a moment.

"Sorry, guys," said Mike Stammer. "I don't know what's wrong with me. I've been hitting OK, but if I don't fix my fielding, I'll get sent down again."

"Hey, there's nowhere down from here," Wayne Zane reminded him.

"Gee, thanks. That makes me feel a lot better."

"Just sayin'," replied Wayne.

7

I worked for a very long time after the game. I didn't want to leave until Dylan did. I didn't want to look like a lollygagging dillydallier.

I rounded up the wet towels, put the equipment away, and swept up sunflower seed shells in the dugout. After a while, I couldn't think of anything else to do. I got dressed to go home. By that time, the players were already gone. Dylan came in just before I left.

"Thanks again for going to the visitors' dugout," I said.

"It was nothing," he said.

"It was something," I said.

"Don't worry about it." He got dressed fast and headed out. I was really sure he was mad at me.

I started to bike home, thought of something, turned around, and caught up with Dylan. I beeped my bike horn at him, and he turned around.

"What now?"

"I'm sorry about what happened at school. If that's what's bothering you, I'm sorry."

"What happened at school?"

"I wanted to brag about being a batboy, but you got to go first. I interrupted you."

"Oh, yeah," Dylan said. "I'm not mad about that."

"So what's bugging you?"

"Oh, man. You're the last one in the world who would understand."

"Understand what? Try me."

"I just don't like baseball."

"What?"

"I think it's boring."

"How could anybody find baseball boring?" I asked.

"I knew you wouldn't understand." Dylan started walking again.

"I'll try!" I said. "Seriously." I pedaled after him. "Just tell me what's boring about it. You have pitchers and batters and home runs and triples and stolen bases and hot boxes and . . . and . . . Hey, how come you have this job if you don't like baseball?"

"My dad said I had to do something this summer besides hang around the house," Dylan replied. "He gave me a few choices, and I picked this one. I figured I'd only have to work half the time, since I wouldn't have anything to do when the Porcupines are on the road."

"So you just called the team up and asked for a job?"

"I sent them a résumé. My dad helped me with it."

"Hey, me too! Did you have to do an interview?"

"Yeah."

"Did you wear a tie?"

"My dad made me, but Wally didn't like it."

"Me too! Did you have to explain the infield fly rule?"

"No, but I could have. I studied. Wally asked me to explain what a balk is."

"Oh." I was glad I didn't get that question. I knew what a balk was, but had trouble explaining it.

"Anyway," Dylan said. "I like hanging out with you. It makes things a little less boring."

"Thanks." I decided I would help Dylan turn into a real fan before the end of the season. How hard could that be when we were so close to the action?

I met Dad on the sidewalk in front of our house. He was walking our dog, Penny. She was happy to see me and barked. I knelt down to scratch her ears.

"I didn't think you'd be back so late," said Dad. "The game was finished two hours ago."

"There's a lot to do afterwards," I explained.

We went inside. Dad unleashed Penny, and she followed me into the living room.

Mom muted the TV. "It looked like you were having fun," she said, "even though the Porcupines lost."

"Yeah. Wait—you were there?"

"We wouldn't have missed it for anything," said Mom.

"Besides," said Dad, "we wanted to make sure you weren't shirking your duties."

"He's so proud of you," Mom said. "He kept nudging the guy next to him and saying, 'That's my boy.'"

"You did it, too," Dad muttered.

• • •

I decided to go to bed early. The Porcupines had a day game tomorrow. And not just any day game, either. It was Kids Get In Free Day. The ballpark would be packed, and a lot of my friends would be there. I wanted to be rested and ready.

I looked at the bookshelf lined with binders and boxes full of baseball cards. I liked baseball cards even before I liked baseball. I liked seeing where players came from and what minor league teams they had played for. Some of my favorite cards had random facts about players that had nothing to do with baseball: It would say that a player's boyhood nickname was Peanut or that his favorite food was Mallomars. When I knew about the guys in the game, the game was more interesting.

That's what Dylan needed, I realized. If he knew the players and their stories, he would *have* to like the game better.

I couldn't drag my whole collection into the locker room. I would have to put all my favorite cards together.

I started pulling binders off the shelf.

A banner hanging high over the gate to Pine City Park read, "KIDS GET IN FREE TODAY!" Below that was a second line: "What's the Big Surprise? Be the First to Know!"

There were Pines fans in the parking lot, grilling hamburgers and waiting for the gates to open. A couple of guys were painting the porcupine statue in front of the ballpark. Workers at the snack stands were heating up oil for waffle fries and mini donuts. Folks from the radio station that broadcast the games were setting up a table on the plaza. They were giving out free porcupine-shaped balls, just like the ones used in the porcupine toss. Inside the ballpark, the field crew were mowing the grass and raking the mound.

Six or seven players were already in the Pines' locker room, kneeling in a half-circle by one of the lockers. I thought I'd walked in on a secret player ritual or an exercise drill.

"Look—he's eating it," said one of the players.

"Of course he's eating it."

I peered over their shoulders and saw a fuzzy brown bunny working on a bit of lettuce in Mike Stammer's outstretched hand.

"Hey, it's a rabbit." What was that all about?

"It was your idea," Mike said, looking up at me. "I got him at the animal shelter this morning. I'm going to let this little guy work his magic on me."

Grumps Humboldt came in and craned his neck to see what was going on. "Why is there a rodent in the locker room?"

"What do you have against rodents, Mister Humboldt?" Lance Pantaño asked. "Our team is named for a rodent."

"It's not a rodent," said Wayne Zane. "It's a lagomorph."

"We're in last place and you fellows are turning this place into a petting zoo," the manager grumbled.

"Lagomorph. Not a rodent. Just sayin'," Wayne mumbled.

"It's only one rabbit," said Mike Stammer. He moved the bunny to a cage by his locker. "I brought him in to help."

"How is that lago-whatsit

going to help us?" Grumps asked. "Is he going to play shortstop?"

"If a rabbit's foot is good luck, why not a whole rabbit?" Mike asked. "Four feet—four times as much luck."

"You can't argue with that," said Wayne Zane. "It's simple math."

"Great," said Grumps. "Next you'll bring a horse in here and tell me it's four times luckier than a horseshoe."

The rabbit hopped into a corner of the cage. I wondered if cleaning its cage would be a batboy-type duty or if Mike would do it.

I stowed my binder on top of my locker and changed into my uniform. I felt a few butterflies in my stomach. There would be a lot of kids at today's game, and a lot of people watching me. What if I messed up?

Dylan came in and noticed the rabbit. "Who's that?" he asked.

"He's our new shortstop," said Grumps. "Can't be any worse than our old one."

"He's cute," said Dylan. He crouched by the cage and let the rabbit sniff his fingertips. Then he reached in between the bars and lightly petted its ears.

Grumps had taped up the day's lineup card on the dugout wall, and I used it to set up the bat rack. It was easy—I just had to put a couple of bats for each player in the rack in the same order they batted. Batting gloves and helmets and mitts went in the bins over the rack.

I finished with that chore and saw that Dylan was still playing with the bunny. He wasn't even in uniform yet.

"You kids want to help out with BP?" Wally shouted from the doorway.

"I guess," said Dylan. He got up slowly and went to get dressed.

I didn't get a chance to show him my cards and start converting him into a baseball fan. Maybe what Dylan really needed was for the players to have big ears and cottontails.

The stands were already full when we ran out to the field for batting practice.

"Hey, look—there he is!" I heard someone shout from the left field bleachers. "Hey, Chad!" I looked up and saw a bunch of kids from class. I waved.

"Where's Dylan?" Oscar called out.

I pointed over to right field.

"Nice uniform!" shouted Ivan.

"Thanks!" I shouted back.

"Hey!" Myung Young, the center fielder,

got my attention. He pointed at home plate.

"I'm working right now!" I reminded my friends, and turned around just in time to see a white bullet coming right at my head. I panicked and froze. Myung leaped in front of me and caught the ball.

"Nice play!" shouted Oscar.

I tried to shrug it off and waited for another ball to come my way.

Sammy Solaris was still in the batter's box, and sent another ball flying. I backed up and kept the ball in front of me, just like I learned in Little League. I fielded this one OK.

"Hey, Chad! Can I have the ball?" Ivan asked.

I shook my head. Wally said we couldn't keep anything or give anything away. He was really clear about it.

"Come on! Please?" Ivan asked.

I glanced around. Nobody seemed to be looking. Besides, it was Kids Get In Free Day. Ivan was a kid. I lobbed the ball into the stands and wheeled around to watch Sammy bat again. He sent a few balls into center field. Myung Young showed off his skills, leaping for one and diving for another. A third hooked foul and was caught by a fan. On Sammy's last swing he sent another ball my way. I fielded it on a bounce.

"Over here!" Oscar shouted. "Throw me the ball!"

"I can't," I shouted back.

"You gave one to Ivan!"

I sighed, and tossed it to him. If some foul balls were fair game, why not a few balls that didn't really make it?

That wasn't how Wally felt about it. He lectured me when I got back to the dugout.

"You know the rules," he said. "Round up

the balls and bring them back. Baseballs don't grow on trees, you know."

"The center part does," said Wayne Zane. "It's made out of cork and rubber. Those are both from trees."

"*Finished* baseballs don't grow on trees," Wally replied. "If they do, Wayne, then plant me a baseball tree."

"I was just sayin'," Wayne mumbled.

"Sorry," I told Wally. "I got excited. Those are friends of mine."

"It's all right this time," he said. "Just don't make a habit of it."

• • •

Mike Stammer came into the dugout carrying the rabbit cage. He set it on the end of the bench.

"Pinch runner?" Myung Young asked.

"Good-luck charm," Mike explained.

"Maybe he can run for me," said Sammy Solaris.

"A tortoise could pinch-run for you," said Wayne Zane.

Sammy glared at him.

"Just sayin'!" said Wayne.

Grumps came into the dugout, saw the rabbit there, and shook his head. "That thing better not chew up the bats," he said.

There was a huge roar from the crowd. Victor Snapp was making an announcement, but I couldn't hear it over the applause. I stepped onto the field to get a better look at what was happening.

Pokey the Porcupine rolled by on a golf cart, and there was a new kid-size mascot with him. The mascot looked really cool! His quills poked out of his head like a punk-rock hairdo, and he had a team shirt on top of his porcupine costume. The sidekick stood on the seat next to Pokey and waved at the fans.

So that was the surprise—and it was great! The Pines had a kid mascot, just in time for Kids Get In Free Day!

Victor Snapp repeated the announcement, "Fans, please welcome to Pine City Park the Porcupines' brand-new junior mascot . . . *Spike!*"

Spike jumped out of the cart and did a handstand and then a cartwheel. He skipped toward the left field seats. He jumped up and slapped hands with every kid who reached out to him. Then he did a little dance while the stereo blasted a classic rock song. He was a big hit.

I noticed Dylan was standing next to me. "The new mascot is great," I said.

"Yeah," he said. "I bet that's more fun than being a batboy."

"Nah," I replied, even though I was thinking the same thing. But only for a moment!

"*Almost* more fun, then," Dylan said.

"Hey, shouldn't you be over helping the Humdingers?" I asked.

"Oh, I was, uh, kind of hoping that you would go to the visitors' dugout today," Dylan replied.

"Oh." It took me about half a second to figure out what was going on. Dylan wanted to stay in the Porcupines' dugout so he could play with that rabbit. Its four feet weren't bringing *me* any luck.

"Yeah, I can do that," I said. It was only fair.

I ran across the infield, veering around the field crew and nearly crashing into Spike.

"Hi, Chad," the junior mascot said.

I was in the visitors' dugout before I remembered that mascots never talked.

Also, how did Spike know my name?

• • •

The Humdingers sent me off to get food. Food was free for players, and I got to jump to the front of the line. I loaded up with hot dogs and pretzels and nachos and started back for the dugout. I took a few wrong steps toward the Porcupines' side before I remembered I was supposed to be going the other way. I spun around and crashed into a big guy in a polo shirt. I dumped the tray all over both of us. I had mustard and ketchup on my uniform. He had cheese sauce all over his shoes.

"Oh, no! Sorry!" I told him. I looked up and realized who it was: Victor Snapp, the Porcupines' official announcer!

He wasn't just the announcer. He was my idol. I wanted to be a sports announcer when I grew up.

Sometimes I practiced at home. "Now batting for the Pine City Porcupines . . . the first baseman . . . Tedddddddddy Larrrrrabeeeee!" I would say. I practiced every name on the roster. I would also practice some of Victor's favorite expressions. "It's a gapper!" he'd say when a ball scooted past an outfielder and rolled to the wall. "It's a goner!" he'd say when a ball cleared the fence.

I'd always wanted to meet Victor Snapp—but not like this.

"Eep! Sorry!" I said.

"Pardon *me*," Mr. Snapp said in the same

booming voice that he used when he was announcing. He went over to the counter to grab a handful of napkins and wipe off his shoes.

I turned around . . . and faced four or five of my classmates. They'd seen the whole thing.

"Wow," said Emily. "That was *epic*."

"Did you do that on purpose?" asked Ellie.

"No way!"

I went back to the snack counter to stock up again, feeling as jinxed as Mike Stammer. Maybe his jinx had rubbed off on me. I'd been nearly creamed by a fly ball right in front of my friends. Wally had yelled at me for giving away practice balls. Dylan had kicked me out of the Porcupines' dugout over a bunny. Now I was covered in ketchup and mustard. If that wasn't being jinxed, I didn't know what was.

11

The worst thing about working in the opponents' dugout was Ernie Hecker. Ernie had the loudest mouth in Pine City. He was even louder than Victor Snapp, and Victor had a speaker system.

Ernie usually sat right above the visiting team's dugout—so he could yell at the opposing players. He also yelled at the umpires, the groundskeepers, the woman who played the organ, and other fans. He even yelled at the Porcupines players sometimes, although he was supposed to be a fan. The only time Ernie was ever quiet was during the national anthem. Sometimes the organ player would play it again in the middle of the game just to shut him up for a few minutes.

The first batter for the Humdingers stepped up to the plate. He reached up before getting into his stance and patted his helmet two or three times.

"Hey, Grankowski!" Ernie shouted. "Afraid your head will fly off?"

Kip Kilgore was pitching for the Pines. He brought his leg way up, kicked, and pitched.

He threw a bullet past the batter.

"Strike!" the umpire called.

The crowd cheered.

"Hey, Kilgore, what are you, a ballerina? Get your leg out of the way so I can see you pitch!" Ernie shouted.

My ears were already hurting.

Grankowski double-tapped his helmet again and got back into his stance.

Kilgore raised his leg high, kicked, and zipped another ball in.

Grankowski swung and missed.

"I think you have a hole in your bat!" Ernie shouted.

Grankowski caught up to the next pitch and sent the ball rolling down the third base line.

"Foul ball, foul ball, foul ball," I chanted. It worked! The ball hooked foul. I leaped out of the dugout to field it—and the ball rolled right between my legs.

"Hey, kid," Ernie shouted. "Does the *BB* stand for Bill Buckner?" A few people near him laughed. Bill Buckner was a famous first baseman. He blew a play that pretty much cost the Red Sox the World Series. It happened years before I was born, but I knew all about it. Everybody who knows baseball knew all about it.

I got the ball and slipped back in the dugout. At least nobody asked me for the ball.

"Nice try," said one of the Humdingers. That just made it worse. Now I had to say "Thanks" to one of the guys who were trying to beat the Porcupines.

"Thanks," I said.

Grankowski bounced the next pitch to short. Mike Stammer moved to get it, stepped on the ball, tripped, and fell flat on his back. The crowd gasped as Grankowski took first.

"Might as well stay down there!" Ernie shouted.

I fetched the bat and put it in the visitors' bat rack, hoping Mike's error wouldn't come back to hurt the Porcupines.

Obviously, the rabbit wasn't working, at least not as a jinx breaker. He seemed to be doing all right as a lettuce-eating lagomorph, though. He was also doing great as Dylan's new best friend.

Mike got up. He didn't seem hurt.

The next batter knocked a ball just left of second base. Mike stuck out his glove, but the ball bounced off the webbing and into center field.

"I told you to stay down there!" Ernie shouted.

Mike punched his glove a couple of times, crouched, and waited for the next batter. I got the bat and brought it back to the dugout.

"Tough way to start a game, huh?" one of the Humdingers asked. It was the same guy who had said "Nice try" earlier.

"Yeah," I agreed.

The next batter rapped the ball to second base. The Pines' George "President" Lincoln threw to first for an easy out.

"He could've turned two," said the Humdinger player.

"Maybe," I replied.

But I knew that Humdinger was right. It was what they call a made-to-order double play. Lincoln could have—should have—thrown the ball to Mike Stammer. Mike would have had to catch the ball, touch second base, and make a clean throw to first. It wasn't easy, but every professional shortstop did it all the time. I gulped. George Lincoln didn't trust Mike anymore! And if the second baseman didn't trust the shortstop to turn a double play, the Porcupines were in big trouble!

The next batter scorched the ball to center field. Myung Young flew and made a diving catch. The runners had taken off with the pitch, and Myung was able to lob the ball to second for a double play. The President fielded the ball at second, stepping in front of Mike to do so.

"Nice play! I wish that guy in center was on my team," said the friendly Humdinger. He grabbed his glove and headed out to left field. I checked the lineup for his name. It was Brian Somerset, a real major leaguer! He was just off the disabled list and getting back up to speed in the minors.

I had Somerset's baseball card. I even had it with me. I didn't know he would be at the game. I could have shown his card to Dylan. The back of the card said, "Brian Somerset started out as a batboy for the Shreveport Captains of the Texas League." I thought Dylan would like that.

I wanted Brian Somerset to sign my card,

but my binder was in the Porcupines' locker room. Pokey and Spike were leading a bunch of little kids through an obstacle course, so I had a few minutes to run and get the card. I just needed an excuse to slip away.

Tommy led off for the Porcupines. He went through the whole routine of checking his laces, pulling up his socks, and rubbing his bat.

"You're batting, not having your picture taken!" Ernie shouted.

I chased down one foul and ignored a chorus of kids begging for the ball. Tommy struck out a few pitches later.

Myung came up. He bounced one toward third base and nearly reached first. It looked like he beat the throw, but the first base umpire called him out. The crowd booed.

"Hey, umpire! What game are you

watching?" Ernie shouted. "The one we're watching, the guy was safe!"

It was Mike's turn to bat.

"I hope you hit better than you field!" Ernie shouted.

Mike took a couple of pitches and then banged a double to left field. The crowd cheered.

Sammy Solaris came up to bat. The crowd cheered and stomped. Sammy was the best hitter on the team. He fouled a ball back into the stands, took a pitch, and then knocked the ball into the outfield.

Mike sprinted, taking a big turn at third and heading home. The Humdinger center fielder fired the ball toward the plate. Mike had plenty of time to score, but he hesitated. He who hesitates is lost, and Mike was definitely lost. The catcher tagged him out. The crowd groaned.

It wasn't even the jinx this time. Mike was jinxed on defense, but he had always been good on offense. He was losing trust in himself, just like the rest of the Porcupines were.

If he didn't break that jinx soon, Mike was done for as a ballplayer.

12

It was the Humdingers' turn to bat again. Brian Somerset was first up. He hit a single and spent most of the inning standing on first base.

I still needed to fetch his baseball card from the Pines' locker room anyway. Too bad I was stuck in the Humdingers' dugout.

The shortstop was chomping on a big wad of gum. Every few seconds he would blow a bubble. He'd let it get bigger and bigger and then . . . POP!

"Could you please knock that off?" asked Grankowski.

"Knock what off?" the shortstop mumbled around his gum.

"Snapping your gum. It's getting on my nerves," Grankowski replied.

"Fine, I'll stop popping bubbles," said the shortstop. He blew a really big bubble, but this time he didn't pop it.

"That's even worse," Grankowski grumbled. He looked away.

The shortstop removed the gum, bubble and all, and carefully attached it to the center of Grankowski's cap.

Every other guy in the dugout cracked up.

"What's going on?" Grankowski reached up and accidentally poked the bubble. POP!

"Great. Now my cap is ruined." He took it off and looked at the blotch of gum.

"Oops," said the shortstop.

This was the perfect chance to go get my binder!

"We've got a bubblegum removal kit," I said. We really did—I'd seen it in the Porcupines' equipment room.

"Go get it!" said Grankowski.

"And get me some more gum," added the shortstop.

I bolted through the Humdingers' locker room, out onto the concourse, and around to the Porcupines' side of the ballpark. I found the gum removal kit first, then ran into the locker room and grabbed my binder.

Wally caught me.

"What are you doing here during the game?"

I was breathing too hard to talk. I made like I was chewing gum, pretended to spit it out and stick it on my own cap, then showed him the spray bottle and scraper.

"Fine, fine. Get back there."

• • •

I went to work cleaning Grankowski's cap.

I remembered my interview with Wally.

Sometimes being a batboy is fun, he'd told me, and sometimes it isn't. He could have added, sometimes it's sticky and gross.

"You shouldn't have to do that," said Brian Somerset.

"It's no big deal," I said. "Hey, can you sign a card for me?" I pointed at the binder. "It's on the fourth page."

"No problem." He found the card and slipped it out, signed it, and put it back. "Nice collection," he said.

"I have a lot more at home," I bragged.

I finished de-gumming the cap and gave it back to Grankowski.

"You're a hero," he said.

The half-inning ended, and the Humdingers went back out to the field. I got my binder to see what Brian Somerset had written on the card.

"For a super batboy from a former batboy!" it said. It was now one of my favorite cards of all time. I decided to move it up front, but I wondered which card to move to make room. I looked carefully at the first page in my binder.

Bill Buckner's card was there. It was one of the cards Uncle Rick had given me. I could see on the card that Buckner's fielding stats were fine. It wasn't fair that he was known for one lousy play. Right next to Buckner's card was a card for Rafael Furcal. The back of Furcal's card said he once turned a triple play all by himself. That's why I put his card in my binder. There's nothing as rare in baseball as an unassisted triple play. It's only happened fifteen times in the major leagues so far.

The funny thing was, Furcal had a lot of errors in his stats. He was a good fielder, but he also made a lot of mistakes. He was the opposite of Bill Buckner. Furcal would always be known for one great defensive play.

Victor Snapp made an announcement: "Kids who want to run the bases after the game, sign up with our new junior mascot, Spike, on the concourse in section E!"

The announcement sent hordes of young kids running to the stairs. It sounded like a herd of very small buffalo stampeding overhead.

"Be right back," I said to the Humdingers in the dugout. I slipped Furcal's baseball card into my front pocket and set off to find Spike the Porcupine.

●　●　●

Little kids crowded around Spike. The junior mascot had a clipboard and wrote down names, but there were so many kids shouting at him that he couldn't keep up. He held up a single finger to mean "one at a time." A kid grabbed his hand and tried to bite it.

I waded through the crowd. "Excuse me. Excuse me," I said. "Official Porcupines business." I pointed at my uniform to show them I was with the team.

"You've got food on your shirt!" one kid reminded me.

"I know. Excuse me."

"*Psst,*" I said to the junior mascot. "*Psst,* Abby."

She couldn't hear me whisper over the mob.

"Hey, Abby!" I shouted.

That got the little porcupine's attention.

"Chad? I can't talk when I'm in costume," Abby said. "Wait a minute—how did you know it was me?"

"Lucky guess . . . and I remembered what you said about your job on the last day of school. Can you please do me a favor? Go to the Pines' dugout and give this to Mike Stammer." I gave Abby the Rafael Furcal baseball card.

"Mike who?"

"Mike Stammer. He's the shortstop."

"He's short?"

"No! He's the—oh, never mind. His name is Mike Stammer. His last name is on his uniform."

Abby took the card, felt around for a pocket, but then realized her porcupine costume didn't have any. She tucked the card into the clip on her board. "OK, but remember, I can't talk to him," she said.

"I know. Thanks!" I left her in the sea of kids and hoped she'd remember Mike's name.

I also hoped that Mike would get what I was trying to tell him. Maybe a baseball card couldn't break the jinx—but maybe it could. He would see that even a player who got a bunch of errors wasn't jinxed on every single play—and if he wasn't jinxed on every play, he wasn't jinxed at all!

13

The Pines were winning by a score of 2–0 at the top of the ninth inning. The closer, Ryan Kimball, was brought in to save the game.

Ryan glared at the Humdinger's batter, Brian Somerset, and spun a crazy breaking ball past him. Ryan had a kooky delivery: His elbows stuck out every which way, and he did a little kick at the end that made it look like he was dancing. His nickname was "Hokey Pokey," but I wouldn't dare call him that to his face. Hokey Pokey or not, the guy could pitch.

Brian swung and missed. Wayne Zane zipped the ball back, and Ryan threw another pitch, hard over the plate. Brian held off that one: Strike two! The crowd started to cheer.

Brian had been nice to me, and it wouldn't hurt the Pines if he just got a base hit. I found myself quietly rooting for him—even if he *was* a Humdinger.

Ryan threw another fastball. Brian knocked it straight over the left field wall. I gulped. I just wanted him to hit a single, not a home run.

"Nice one," I told him when he got back to the dugout. I had to be polite. I didn't high-five him, though. I was still a Pine City Porcupines' fan all the way. I had to draw the line somewhere.

"Thanks," Brian said. "I got lucky."

The next Humdinger batter walked, and the batter after that bunted. It was a really good bunt that rolled along the third base line and stopped dead. The runner from first reached second, and the batter reached first. Now the tying run was in scoring position, and the go-ahead run was on base. There was still nobody out. I couldn't watch. I pulled the brim of my hat low so I couldn't see.

I heard a strike called, and then there was the crack of the bat.

The crowd roared, louder than I'd ever heard. I lifted the brim of my cap and saw the base runners walking back toward the dugout.

The Pines were swarming Mike Stammer!

"That was something!" said Brian Somerset. "I've never seen anything like it."

They showed the replay on the big screen. The Humdinger batter lined the pitch right up the middle. It was the kind of ball that goes so fast and straight that people call it a "frozen rope." Mike Stammer jumped four feet high and caught the ball.

That was one out.

Mike touched second base before the base runner could get back to the bag.

That made two outs.

Meanwhile, the player from first was still running toward second; all Mike had to do was reach out and touch him.

That was three outs.

An unassisted triple play! The rarest play in baseball!

The replay ran again and again, so I watched it again and again. It was a two-second masterpiece: catch, touch, and tag in one motion. It was a great, great play. There was no way Mike Stammer was jinxed.

They showed the Porcupines' dugout on the big screen too. The bench players all high-fived each other. Even Dylan got five, and Grumps cracked the first smile I had seen from him. I wished like anything I was over there.

Mike ran toward the visitors' dugout. The Humdingers watched in surprise. Was he coming to taunt them?

"Hey, Chad the batboy!" Mike called.

"What a great play!" I told him.

"The little porcupine gave me this." He pulled the card out. "It came with a note that said, 'This is from Chad the batboy.'"

"Yeah, I thought it might help break the jinx."

"It sure did!" said Mike. "Can I keep it? I mean, now I'm scared *not* to have it—you know?"

"Uh . . . sure," I answered. It was hard to give up the card, but that was better than rejinxing a guy.

"I'll get you a new card," Mike said. "Tell you what, you can keep the ball." He was still

holding the baseball he'd turned the triple play with.

"Wow! Thanks."

"This ball has to be good luck," Mike added.

"Not for us," said Brian Somerset.

"Can you sign it for me?" I asked Mike.

"Of course."

I tossed him a pen. I made a terrible throw, but he caught it anyway.

• • •

I helped the Humdingers put their things away for the night. When I went back onto the field, there was still a long, ragged line of kids waiting to run the bases. A couple of the kids were talking about Mike's play and acting it out.

"Wasn't that awesome?"

"Yeah," Dylan replied.

"First unassisted triple play in Prairie League history!" I heard one of them say.

Spike pointed at each kid when it was his or her turn to run the bases. He—I mean, she—waved at me as I passed.

"I can't talk right now!" Abby said. "I'm in costume!"

"That's all right. Neither can I."

"I gave that guy the card, though!" she said.

"I know. Thanks!"

The Porcupines' locker room was practically empty. Dylan was playing with the rabbit. The locker room was in good shape, so at least he had finished his duties before taking a bunny break.

"Is Mike still around?" I asked.

"I don't think so. All the guys wanted to take him out to celebrate his big play."

"Must have been fun to be in the dugout when it happened," I said.

"It was."

Dylan should have been a lot more excited.

I still planned on turning him into a big-time baseball fan. Good thing I had all summer to do it.

"Looks like Mike left his rabbit behind," I said.

"It's my rabbit now," said Dylan. "Mike said I could keep him because we hit it off so well."

"Do your parents know you're coming home with a rabbit?"

"Sure they do. They're coming to pick us up. We have two rabbits already, so he'll fit right in."

"He's cute," I said. "Have you named him yet?"

"I'm still thinking about it," he said. "Any ideas?"

"How about . . . Jinx?"

"I like that! I like it a lot!"

"Thanks. It just kind of came to me."

About the Author

Kurtis Scaletta's previous books include *Mudville*, which *Booklist* called "a gift from the baseball gods" and named one of their 2009 Top 10 Sports Books for Youth. Kurtis lives in Minneapolis with his wife and son and some cats. He roots for the Minnesota Twins and the Saint Paul Saints. Find out more about him at www.kurtisscaletta.com.

About the Artist

Eric Wight was an animator for Disney, Warner Bros., and Cartoon Network before creating the critically acclaimed *Frankie Pickle* graphic novel series. He lives in Doylestown, Pennsylvania, and is a diehard fan of the Philadelphia Phillies and the Lehigh Valley Iron Pigs. You can check out all the fun he is having at www.ericwight.com.